GARY PAULSEN

MUDSHARK

A YEARLING BOOK

Copyright © 2009 by Gary Paulsen

All rights reserved. Published in the United States by Yearling, an imprint of Random House Children's Books, a division of Random House, Inc., New York. Originally published in hardcover in the United States by Wendy Lamb Books, an imprint of Random House Children's Books, a division of Random House, Inc., New York, in 2009.

Yearling and the jumping horse design are registered trademarks of Random House, Inc.

Visit us on the Web! www.randomhouse.com/kids
Educators and librarians, for a variety of teaching tools, visit us at
www.randomhouse.com/teachers

The Library of Congress has cataloged the hardcover edition of this work as follows:
Paulsen, Gary.
Mudshark / Gary Paulsen.   p.   cm.
Summary: Principal Wagner confidently deals with a faculty washroom crisis, a psychic parrot, and a terrorizing gerbil, but when sixty-five erasers go missing, he enlists the help of the school's best problem solver and locator of lost items, twelve-year-old Lyle Williams, aka Mudshark.
ISBN 978-0-385-74685-4 ((trade hc) : alk. paper) — ISBN 978-0-385-90922-8 ((lib. bdg.) : alk. paper) — ISBN 978-0-375-89255-4 (e-book)
[1. Problem solving—Fiction. 2. Lost and found possessions—Fiction.
3. Schools—Fiction. 4. Humorous stories.] I. Title. II. Title: Mudshark.
PZ7.P2843Mu 2009   2008033271

ISBN 978-0-553-49464-8 ((pbk.) : alk. paper)

Printed in the United States of America
10 9 8 7 6 5 4
First Yearling Edition

To Leo Lashock
with gratitude

MUDSHARK

1

This is the principal. *Would the custodian please report to the faculty restroom with a plunger . . . no, wait . . . a shovel and a plunger? And has anybody seen the gerbil from room two oh six?*

The Mudshark was cool.

Not because he said he was cool or knew he was or thought it. Not because he tried or even cared.

He just was.

Kind of tall, kind of thin, with a long face, brown eyes and hair and a quick smile that jumped out and went back. When he walked down a hall he didn't just walk, he seemed to move as a part of the hall. He'd suddenly appear out of nowhere, as if he'd always been there.

Wasn't there.

Then there.

His real name was Lyle Williams and for most of his twelve-year-old life people had just called him Lyle.

But one day, when he'd been playing Death Ball—a kind of soccer mixed with football and wrestling and rugby and mudfighting, a citywide, generations-old obsession that had been banned from school property because of, according to the principal, Certain Insurance Restrictions and Prohibitions Owing to Alarming Health Risks Stemming from the Inhalation and Ingestion of Copious Amounts of Mud—he'd been tripped. Everyone thought he was down for the count, flat on his back, covered in mud. Just then, a runner-kicker-wrestler-mudfighter came too close to him, streaking downfield with the ball, and one of Lyle's hands snaked out and caught the runner by an ankle.

"So fast, it was like a mudshark," Billy Crisper

said later. He always watched the animal channel. "Mudsharks lie in the mud and when something comes by, they grab it so fast that even high-speed cameras can't catch it. I didn't even see his hand move, I didn't see so much as a blur."

After that game, no one called him Lyle.

Mudshark's agility had been honed at home, courtesy of his triplet baby sisters—Kara, Sara and Tara. Once they started crawling, his father said that all heck broke loose, because nothing moves faster than a tiny, determined toddler heading toward a breakable or swallowable object. If Mudshark had only had one little sister or maybe even two, his reflexes wouldn't have been so keen, but living under the same roof as three mobile units at one time had increased his range of motion and speed exponentially.

One night after dinner when they were about seven months old, the babies had been placed on a blanket on the floor and were playing with soft toys. Mudshark was doing his homework at the desk in the corner of the family room and his parents were

3

watching the news and, frankly, dozing on the couch.

Out of the corner of his eye, Mudshark saw a pink flash.

His head whipped around. Two babies were sitting on the blanket, looking toward the door to the hallway. Two, but not three. His parents were half asleep and he didn't want to disturb them. As he leapt silently to his feet and took a step toward the door, he saw two pink streaks darting past him in the same direction. Mudshark reached out and grabbed both babies by the back of their overalls as they crawled after their more adventurous sister. He scooped them up and tucked one under each arm in one fell swoop, heading out of the room toward the rogue baby.

Down the hall toward the kitchen, he saw a little rosebud-covered bottom (a quick glance at the faces he had clutched under his arms told him that Tara had made the first break) rounding the corner to the guest room. He took long strides toward her, Kara and Sara cooing at the jouncy ride. When he got to the guest room, he stared down at Tara, who had found one of the dog's squeezy toys and was happily gumming it (*EEY-ah, EEY-ah . . .*). Three babies, two arms.

He shifted the two girls he was holding to his left side, sliding his arm through their overall straps as if he were slinging a backpack over his forearm. They hung there, gurgling, while he bent over and plucked Tara off the floor.

Mudshark and his wriggling crew returned to the family room, where his parents slept peacefully, unaware that the triplets had discovered mobility.

From that moment on, Mudshark did everything he could to anticipate their moves and keep them out of trouble. He stood guard between the triplets and electrical outlets (there had been a close call with Tara, a Barbie doll and a surge protector), the dog bowl (Sara was especially fond of kibble) and the cat box (Mudshark made a flying leap across the room the first time he saw Kara sitting next to the litter box, reaching a small hand toward the mysterious clumps she saw. He snatched her up before she connected). Yes, he owed his speed and attention to detail to Kara, Sara and Tara.

But the way he moved wasn't why Mudshark was cool.

And it wasn't his clothes. Sometimes his outfit fit in with the way everybody else dressed and sometimes it didn't. Once, he wore a green wool sweater that had a yellow leather diamond stamped with the head of a poodle in the middle of the chest. It was as ugly as broken teeth chewing rotten meat, but by the end of the day everybody in school wished they had a green wool sweater with a yellow leather diamond and a poodle on it, too.

That's how cool Mudshark was.

It didn't matter to Mudshark what they called him or that he wasn't allowed to play Death Ball anymore because of how badly he'd frightened the other players with his fast moves (Death Ball was not known to require cunning or quickness, just the brute force and raw grit necessary to last the four quarters of, as parents and other adults shudderingly referred to it, That Game). Mudshark knew cool wasn't in how you moved or a name or clothes or whether or not you were asked to play on anyone's team.

It was all in the way your thoughts ran through your mind, the way you managed the flow of electrical charges jumping from one brain cell to another to form ideas.

That's what makes somebody who they are. And that's why Mudshark was so cool.

He *thought*.

While everyone else was hanging out or goofing off or playing video games or listening to music or watching TV or walking down the hallway in a funk or texting each other or surfing the Net, he was observing the people and objects and sights and scenes around him.

Thinking.

Once, when he was just five and a half years old, he went up to his mother and said:

"Mom, I think *all* the time."

"About what?"

"Everything." Deep breath, let it out, sigh.

"What are you thinking about right now?"

"Fingernails grow exactly four times faster than toenails, but it's not like we need toenails because we don't even use them for scratching and did you know that an octopus doesn't even *have* toenails . . ." He sighed again, and as he turned to walk away, he said, "It makes a man think."

He also read all the time. His mother was the lead research coordinator at the public library, and from the time he was very tiny, she'd brought him to work with her, setting him on the floor behind her desk with a stack of books she'd absentmind-edly pulled from the nearest shelf—never picture books or easy readers, but books on astronomy and astrophysics and the history of democracy and the rise and fall of ancient civilizations. He'd learned to read before he went to kindergarten and was always carrying two or three books with him. He only had to read a page once to be able to quote from it word for word.

As he grew older, his memory became better be-cause of the way he learned to pay attention to every sight, smell, taste and sound every minute of every day. As with any skill, practice made him more proficient, and over time, he'd developed a nearly photographic memory.

Eventually people noticed his knack for quoting obscure facts and remembering tiny details, and when a kid at school had a question or problem, someone would say "Ask Mudshark."

"Hey, Mudshark," Markie McCorkin said, "I lost my homework!"

And Mudshark remembered him sitting by the steps in front of the school where two small kids had been playing with a ball, a yellow ball, that they'd thrown in the bushes back of where Markie sat. One of them had accidentally kicked Markie's orange folder so that his homework papers, held together with a red paper clip, fell out of the folder while he was telling Todd DeClouet about the new tires on his bicycle and how well they gripped in dirt, although not as well as he'd thought they might.

And Markie ran to the front bushes and sure enough, his homework was there. Exactly where Mudshark had said it would be.

Annie Shaw had unfortunately eaten the Anchovy–

Grape Jelly Turnover Surprise in the cafeteria and asked Mudshark what to do.

He told her she needed to lie quietly until the spins stopped and that she should go to the school nurse right this very minute because the nurse's car insurance payments had been reduced since she never drove over eleven miles an hour, and she would be in such a good mood that she'd give Annie a pass to miss class, even though she usually held the passes back like they were made of gold. *Her* gold. From her teeth.

And Mudshark knew all this because he had overheard the nurse on the phone and seen her car insurance papers on her desk when he'd given her his updated immunization record.

He also knew that there was serious talk about the cook being sent to a Quiet Place for an Indeterminate Time if her recipes didn't start becoming less . . . creative. The nurse was alarmed. Every day there was a line of pale and shaky students sitting in her waiting room, clutching small pails and groaning.

The cool thing about Mudshark was that he not only *had* information, he knew how to *use* it.

10

One day he came back to his locker to discover that somebody had taped a sign to it:

THE MUDSHARK DETECTIVE AGENCY
Problems solved and
items found

He smiled and straightened the sign so it was perfectly level.

This is the principal. Would the custodian please report to the cafeteria with a shovel and a bucket and some extra-strength, reinforced garbage bags? And would those people late for assembly refrain from being late in the future? And if you see the gerbil, would you please try to herd it toward room two oh six?

One of the Death Ball players was a boy named Risdon Risdon. His first and last name were the same, it was said, because his father had also played a lot of Death Ball when he was young and had gotten too used to hearing every call repeated.

Risdon Risdon lost his right shoe while walking down the hallway and had continued walking for quite some time before discovering that (a) he didn't have a shoe and (b) he had no idea where he was going in the first place.

Hard-core Death Ball players were always losing articles of apparel and getting lost because they didn't pay much attention to anything besides the game. But Risdon Risdon was a legend in his own time because he had once failed to find the cafeteria while both double doors were open and people were yelling at him as he walked past.

Somehow, though, Risdon Risdon knew enough to go looking for Mudshark in the library, where so many important things happened.

Mudshark looked up from his book in surprise as Risdon Risdon limped over to him. It was of course nothing short of astonishing that Risdon Risdon was in the library in the first place, considering that Death Ball players spent all their free time during the school day in the cafeteria hunched over notebooks, tinkering with the brackets for the play-offs and carb-loading for strength and endurance.

Risdon Risdon glared down at his feet and bellowed, "Yo, Mud! My shoe is not here. On my right foot, dude. It escaped or something. Got any idea what happened to it? 'Cause I can't go to practice without both shoes."

Mudshark knew that Risdon Risdon's shoe was by locker seventy-four on the right side of the hallway, where Mudshark had seen it flop, toe in to the wall, after third period when Risdon Risdon had become mesmerized by the sight of Amanda Gatto's gleaming hair and had tripped.

Risdon Risdon shuffled off to retrieve his shoe and, he hoped, catch another glimpse of Amanda and her shiny hair while the rest of the students in the library murmured quietly among themselves that Mudshark had a sixth sense or a third eye.

3

This is the principal. *Would the custodian please bring a rag and a strainer and a set of tongs to the faculty restroom? And would whoever drew the picture of George Washington on the sidewalk with chalk please refrain from drawing that particular picture? George Washington, the Father of Our Country, did not wear shorts, have tattoos and chest hair, or smoke cigars. At least I don't think he did. And also refrain from startling the gerbil. When frightened, he reverts to a wild state and looks for a burrow to hide in, and since there are no burrows in the school building he will seek any dark hole. Thank you.*

Somewhere Up There, the higher levels of school administration decided that every classroom should have a live science project. Word came down asking for suggestions. A few were downright frightening, but the letter that received the most attention and prompted the subsequent hiring of a child psychologist whose job it was to visit classrooms throughout the district looking for Potential Cries for Help from Disaffected Youth read, "Body parts could be gathered from city morgues and, using duct tape and the clever manipulation of electricity, a human being could be manufactured."

The school board ultimately decided: crayfish.

Packages of fertilized crayfish eggs arrived at Mudshark's school. They were placed in tanks of water so the crayfish would hatch and grow and young people could then understand the Miracle of Life as seen through the cycle of: boy crayfish meets girl crayfish, and then . . .

It turned out that the main lesson crayfish had to teach was Reproduction and Multiplication of a Species because crayfish are really good at making babies. Pretty soon the classrooms at Mudshark's school were full of glass tanks, teeming with the Miracle of Life—two hundred sixty-five thousand, three hundred and seventeen miracles, to be exact.

The custodian was constantly trying to fit new tanks into the rooms, and everyone hoped that he was garnering huge overtime pay for the weekend and school vacation visits he made to clean the tanks and feed the crayfish, lest they die—which they would, an unfortunate and reeking discovery made immediately following the first three-day weekend of the school year.

So much Life made everyone nervous.

Kids got edgy. They moved their desks together in the center of the room. The teachers moved their desks in, too, and everyone huddled together, warily eyeing the numerous glass tanks that soon surrounded them, lining the walls of each and every classroom.

The custodian was looking haggard, since he had no time off.

So while it might be said that the Crayfish

Project was not a spectacular success—indeed, some teachers needed therapy after the horror of disposing of thousands of dead and decaying crayfish—there were some benefits.

Young people did learn a lot about the Inevitable Cycle of Life, which was sure to help them as they matured and got jobs as bankers and lawyers and car engine designers, then planned the sizes of their own families and immediately had their house pets spayed or neutered. There were also many new recipes for crayfish gumbo on the Internet.

One of the more interesting and long-lasting side effects of the crayfish experiment was that the librarian, Ms. Underdorf, decided to turn her library into a small, personal zoo.

There are many ways to describe Ms. Underdorf.

She was brilliant and joyous and she believed—probably correctly—that libraries contain the answers to all things, to *everything*, and that if you can't find the information you seek in the library, then such information probably does not exist in this or any parallel universe now or ever to be known.

She was thoughtful and kind and she always believed the best of everybody. She was, above all else, a master librarian and knew where to find any book on any subject in the shortest possible time.

And she was wonderfully unhinged. So when the School Administration Science Experiment Directive came down about crayfish, she embraced it with an enthusiasm any educational administrator would have found rewarding.

If a couple of crayfish were good, she thought, looking around at all the empty space in her library that suddenly seemed to cry out for cages and aquariums and terrariums, then other examples of more exotic living creatures would be better.

And so the Amazing Armadillo.

This is the principal. *Would the custodian please report to the faculty restroom with a large stick, safety goggles and a respirator mask? And would whoever took the erasers from room two oh three please return them and refrain from removing erasers in the future? Also, while it is loose, and in spite of what I said in the last announcement, the gerbil is not, per se, a wild animal and will not, repeat, will not attack. So please refrain from screaming or otherwise panicking should you see said gerbil.*

Ms. Underdorf bought an armadillo from a man on a street corner who said he was a professional armadillo salesman from Texas. Since Ms. Under-dorf believed in everybody, she took him at his word and happily brought the little armadillo to school, sleeping soundly, she thought, rolled up in wood shavings in the corner of its glass tank.

She named it Sparky.

Sparky the Amazing Armadillo.

Ms. Underdorf spent long hours cooing soft words over Sparky's tank to help him have sweet dreams, because her research indicated that these particular armadillos were nocturnal. But when she asked the custodian about Sparky's nights, he said Sparky wasn't any more active in the evening hours, when the custodian was there to clean the library.

Ms. Underdorf never noticed that she was the only person in school who paid any attention to Sparky; after a curious glance by the student popula-tion the week he arrived, no one ventured near his table. The explosion of crayfish had curbed their in-terest in animal behavior.

After a while Ms. Underdorf became concerned because Sparky never unrolled and didn't even waken to eat the special lumps of insects she supplied weekly. Armadillos were supposed to love those lumps. One day, when this had been going on for about four weeks, Mudshark noticed that, although Sparky wasn't eating, the spider population of the library was incredibly well fed. He wandered over to Sparky's tank and watched a line of spiders drop in, wrap up Sparky's food and scramble up the sides of the glass tank, stolen dinner in tow.

Mudshark took a close look at Sparky, reaching into the tank to nudge him. Mudshark's eyes widened in surprise.

Mudshark waited until he and Ms. Underdorf were the only people in the library. Then he said carefully, "Uh, Ms. Underdorf. Did you notice that Sparky is . . . um . . . special?"

"Of course he's special! Why, he's downright amazing; he was one of four identical babies born in his litter—all armadillos are born four at a time from one egg. Isn't that cunning?"

"Uh, no. I mean yes, that's clever, very utilitarian, and my family has an appreciation of the multiple-birth phenomenon, as you well know, but what I was talking about, specifically, was that Sparky seems to have, well, it looks to me like a brass clasp is holding his stomach contents in place."

Ms. Underdorf peered intently at Sparky. Mudshark's nudge had flipped him on his side and out of the burrow of wood shavings.

"Well, I'll be . . . ," she said. "Would you look at that! It's a purse! Sparky is actually a purse. Fine observation, Lyle." She beamed proudly at Mudshark. And then she reached in, plucked Sparky out of the glass tank and snapped open the clasp. "Oh, look! A penny. This *is* my lucky day. Thank you, Lyle, for bringing this to my attention." She smiled at Mudshark before taking Sparky to her office and unloading the contents of her old handbag into her new one.

Although Ms. Underdorf was thrilled with her new purse, she still wanted interesting and educational creatures in the library for the betterment of her students.

And so she bought a parrot.

5

This is the principal. _Would the custodian please report to the faculty restroom with a plastic shield, a hazardous waste suit and a large container of pepper spray? Also, whoever took the erasers out of room two oh two, please return them and refrain from removing erasers from two oh two in the future. Also refrain from taking erasers from two oh four. Thank you. Oh, and the gerbil was seen near the vice principal's office—she said it was "scurrying, very ratlike." You should not try to pick it up if it is, indeed, a rat. I repeat: Refrain from picking up rats. Thank you._

The parrot sat completely silent for the better part of a week—so still and quiet that Mudshark thought Ms. Underdorf might have bought it from the same man who sold her Sparky the Amazing Armadillo/kicky new everyday handbag.

But after a week or so, the parrot burped, coughed, scratched a million empty birdseed shells onto the floor, emitted a sound that should have been accompanied by methane, looked at Ms. Underdorf and said:

"Hey, babe, what's happening?"

The parrot seemed to know that he lived in a library; he spoke in a near whisper. Gradually, people realized that he seemed to speak several different languages, or at least it sounded as if he did. Marly Lipinski, for some unknown reason, swore he was reciting off-color limericks in ancient Sanskrit. Of course nobody understood the language anyway, so it didn't matter how racy the poems were.

Other than the incessant belching, the parrot fit right in to Ms. Underdorf's library. She didn't mind the burps or the potentially dirty words because they were, she announced, Proof of Life, and, after Sparky, that was good enough for her.

When the bird had been in Ms. Underdorf's care for just over a month, Betty Crimper came in to the library and asked if anybody had seen her paper on how to make salve out of lard. She had been working on the project for quite a long time, buying pound blocks of lard at the grocery and mixing the lard with what she called "experimental chemicals."

Betty was always doing one experiment or another, looking for a Miracle Cure or Amazing Beauty Potion that would make her Rich and Famous, or at least Rich.

She posted a sign on her locker reading: TEMPORARY HOME OF THE FUTURE BETTY CRIMPER RESEARCH AND DEVELOPMENT LABORATORY.

And except for the time when she tried to bottle Odors to Repel and they had to close down the entire north end of the school after she dropped a small jar in the hall, her experiments hadn't been too dramatic. Betty had packed that jar full of something her cat had dragged in, which she had "cured" in the sun. As she watched the hazmat team herd the students out into the front yard, she'd made a careful note in her lab notebook:

> The curing process went on a bit too long, leading to surprising intensity. General population not ready for Odors to Repel; contact United States Marine Corps. Possible use as weapon?

Her new lard salve, though, seemed to do little damage except to draw flies. This meant that the Death Ball players, who used Betty's salve as muscle balm, walked around in clouds of insects. The players' eyes watered uncontrollably when they used the stuff, but they swore that Betty's concoction was the best bruise medication they'd ever tried.

Then came the day when she rushed into the library and cried, "Has anyone seen my lard recipe?"

"Why don't you ask Mud—" somebody started to say, but before the sentence was finished the parrot belched, squawked and said:

"Check the window ledge in the girls' rest-room."

Mudshark, who was there (of course, he was always in the library), turned to look at the parrot, frowned and then said to Betty, "He's right, you should go look."

So Betty found her paper on the ledge, where it had fallen out of her notebook when she washed her hands after science the day before. Betty had become compulsive about washing her hands after working in the lab following the Episode with the Itching Scabs.

As curious as it was that a parrot should speak logically and not just mimic what he'd heard a person say, and that a mere bird could help somebody find something, the incident passed largely unnoticed by everyone other than Mudshark. He spent a good deal of the rest of the day gazing thoughtfully at the parrot. Later that same week, Clyde Damper was in the library and whispered that he'd lost a book. Before anyone could say, before anyone could even think *Ask Mudshark*, the parrot belched, squawked and said:

"On the bench, by the coach's office."

Clyde, surprised, turned to Mudshark, who was observing the bird. Mudshark looked at Clyde, shrugged and said, "He's right."

Clyde found the book sitting right where the parrot, and Mudshark, had said it would be. Clyde had collected the previous day's attendance sheets from each teacher and taken them to the office earlier that morning and had dropped them all outside Coach's office, setting the book down while he gathered the papers from the floor.

Twice now the bird had known where to find something even though it never left the library.

"I think," Clyde said to his friends, "that bird is special. He has powers. Maybe . . . he's psychic."

By the end of the day the word was all over school.

First: the parrot in the library was psychic.

And second: the parrot could out-think Mudshark.

This is the principal. *Would the custodian please report to the faculty restroom with a long plank? And whoever took the erasers from room two oh eight, please return them. Seriously, a lot of erasers are missing. Please return them. Also please refrain from forming hunting parties to hunt the gerbil. He simply gets frightened and panics and I don't think any of us want to revisit the sound we heard when he ran up Mr. Patterson's pants leg, do we? Luckily the gerbil was not injured, although he escaped again, and Mr. Patterson will return to school day after tomorrow once he has regained his . . . composure. Thank you.*

It shouldn't have bothered Mudshark, shouldn't have rattled his cool, this parrot.

Life, after all, wasn't about out-thinking birds. But it annoyed him a little. Mudshark had gotten used to being the go-to guy in school, and he didn't want to share that position with a bird. Especially a burping bird.

He had a bigger issue than the parrot, though: Something was going on at school, something strange, and he couldn't put his finger on just what felt . . . wrong. As he did with any new thing he wanted to understand, he settled back and waited for his thoughts to become clear.

While waiting, he went to school, watched the season-ending Death Ball play-offs, ate dinner with his parents and broke up a food fight among his sisters.

The girls were separated from each other at the dinner table—Mom, Dad and Mudshark each took charge of one, playing one-on-one defense with the triplets, much like the Death Ball championship team. The physical separation kept the girls from grabbing each other, eating off each other's plates or complaining about the fairness of portion sizes. But instead they used the distance between them to toss food at each other. Mudshark never missed a bite as he raised a hand to snag a dinner roll that Tara had hurled at Sara or to right the glass of milk that Kara had tipped when she flung a pork chop at Tara.

His mother and father didn't seem to notice the food flying across the table—they were engrossed in a discussion of library funding. So Mudshark was left to contain the damage.

After dinner, he rested up by working on his bicycle. Mudshark had learned that a bike is the most efficient way to use human energy to move the body forward. He spent many hours improving his bike's efficiency—lubricating the bearings, cleaning and oiling the chain, perfecting his pedaling technique so that one push on a level street would move him forty yards.

And all the time, he waited.

Waited for the knowledge he needed to figure out what was going on at school.

Mudshark was sitting in the back of a study room the next morning, letting the uneasy thoughts rumble around in his mind, when he saw Emily Davidson pull her gym uniform out of her backpack and swipe it across the blackboard, where she was working on math problems with her study group.

Erasers.

There it was.

Erasers.

Every day more erasers were missing, and although it had seemed like a prank, like the free-range gerbil, somehow Mudshark knew there was more to it; something important was happening with the stolen erasers.

He solved two more thought events while he kept thinking about erasers.

First, Willamena Carson had lost her mind, or rather her brain, and asked Mudshark to find it. Willamena was a perfectly normal twelve-year-old girl who was forever losing her brain. She had decided a few months back that she was destined to be a doctor, and somewhere along the way, she had acquired a model of a human skull, which she studied constantly. At least everybody *hoped* it was a model. Nobody wanted to think that a twelve-year-old girl with a bouncy black ponytail would run around school carrying a real human skull.

Willamena carried the skull in a bowling bag everywhere she went, and when she had nothing else to do, she would pull it out and examine it. The top could be lifted off, and a plastic model of a brain was nestled inside.

"It's plastic," Willamena told everyone, her ponytail bouncing. "If it was real, it would get all runny. Decomposition is bad for brains."

Willamena's brain often fell out of the skull as she made her way through the day, and it turned up in some strange places. The back of a police car, the front pew of the Methodist church, an aisle seat at the movies and the Dumpster to the rear of the Juicy Burger stand had all been graced with Willamena's lost brain. Mudshark always figured out a logical reason: her uncle was a police officer and she had ridden in his squad car, she had gone to the Methodist church with a friend during a weekend sleepover, she'd gone to the movies with her grandmother, and she had been looking near the Dumpster for rats to photograph for a science project.

Most recently, Mudshark had told her she would find her brain bobbing in the shallow end of the town pool, where it was terrifying some little kids who'd heard it was a man-eating brain fish. Willamena had taken her skull swimming in the deep end and had not seen her brain fall out, but Mudshark had heard the children screaming from the bicycle repair shop across the street.

The second thought event was when Kyle Robertson made his father's brand-new, only-one-day-old car disappear.

Kyle had wanted to be a magician his entire life. Every waking moment of every day, he studied books on magic and—most important—on the art of misdirection. This means making the audience focus on the wrong thing so it fails to see how the magician pulls off the trick.

Kyle had had early successes with making various

things disappear and reappear—notably his neighbor Helen Cartwright's huge cat, Toby. Toby finally got fed up with being disappeared and started to perform a lobotomy on Kyle, so Kyle moved on to things that didn't hiss and spray pee: his sisters' favorite dolls, clothing, bicycles, coins, school lunches, books, a gym teacher's whistle and clipboard, three and a half lockers and, once, a watermelon and a large potato.

Kyle soon tired of these easy bits of magic and went looking for bigger and better feats of misdirection, searching for the major, the truly giant accomplishment, and was frustrated, until . . .

Until his father bought a new car.

Kyle's father had spent hours going over consumer guides and dragging his family from one car dealership to the next to test-drive every make and model in the region before finally picking the *exact* car that he wanted, the car of his dreams, the car that would get the best mileage per gallon with the least upkeep and maintenance and the strongest, most ironclad, waterproof, consumer-friendly warranty.

Kyle promptly disappeared the car.

Disappeared it *too* well. Even *he* couldn't find it.

This was, clearly, the most successful act of magical misdirection Kyle had ever done, or probably would do for the rest of his life, which, according to his angry father, might be very short indeed if he did not produce the car.

Now.

So Kyle, talking fast, called Mudshark and begged him to come over. Mudshark found the car, as good as new, around the corner and down the block. Mudshark was kind enough not to give away the secret of Kyle's trick, which was actually not misdirection at all but an unlucky combination of his attempting the trick with the help of (1) his sixteen-year-old cousin (or, as Kyle referred to her, "my lovely assistant Kimmie"), who drove off in the car and forgot where she'd parked it, and (2) Kyle's dad's spare set of keys, which would no longer be kept on a peg by the back door after what soon became known in Kyle's house as That Darnfool Magic Nonsense with My Brand-new Car That I'd Hardly Driven Yet.

"See?" Kyle told his father. "It was never really gone in the first place. It was all just sleight of hand—"

"If you ever do it again," his father said, "I will direct *my* hand to a part of your anatomy so hard you won't sit down for three months."

"Yes, Dad." Kyle sounded meek, even though he was secretly wondering what he could possibly do to top this one.

And Mudshark went back to his thinking, which was more and more centered around one word:

Erasers.

7

This is the principal. Would the custodian please report to the faculty restroom with a large drum of disinfectant and a personal flotation device? Also, would whoever took the erasers from room two oh nine please return them? This holds true for all the other erasers, all sixty-five currently missing. Would whoever took them please refrain from taking any more and return all the missing ones to the appropriate rooms at once? There is nothing new to report about the gerbil except that he is still somewhere in the building. Will Mud . . . Lyle Williams please report to the principal's office? Immediately.

While one part of Mudshark's mind was working on *erasers*, another part was trying to figure out the parrot.

Most of the school had come to believe in the power and knowledge of the bird. Soon after the parrot's first successful solution, faculty and staff started asking him for winning lottery numbers, students begged for predictions on upcoming grades and answers to the chemistry midterm, most of the Death Ball players wanted to know the results of sporting events—including a cow-pie–throwing contest in Kansas City—and the custodian quietly whispered a request about where to find true love.

The library was rapidly becoming the most popular room in the school, a fact that pleased Ms. Underdorf no end. Kids came in and pretended to look for a book, always on a subject that took them near the parrot's cage. Then they would sidle up to the bird and whisper a question.

The parrot would sit, eyes closed, as if pretending that no one was there.

The bird never answered questions about lottery

tickets or test answers or sports teams or even true love, but when someone wanted to find a lost item, he would emit the now-famous belch, squawk and reveal where the object could be found.

He wasn't always right, not like Mudshark, but he was, after all, a *parrot* and he was correct often enough that word spread through the school of his superpowers. The more people talked about him, the more they believed in him. And when Harvey Blenderman guessed accurately that Darryl F. Fergesen would win the Kansas City cow-pie–throwing contest rubber-gloved hands down, Harvey gave credit to the parrot even though the bird hadn't said a word.

Everyone thought it was just a matter of time before the bird shot Mudshark down as the undisputed answer champion. As much as kids liked and admired Mudshark and had come to rely on him for help, they secretly agreed that having a psychic parrot living in their school library was far more interesting than having a know-it-all twelve-year-old.

All of this was on Mudshark's mind when the PA system crackled to life:

Will Mud . . . Lyle Williams please report to the principal's office? Immediately.

As he made his way to Mr. Wagner's office, a wave of doom and gloom swamped him. Any time a person was ordered to report to the principal *immediately*, bad news followed.

Mudshark was ushered past the school secretary—a thin, always-smiling woman of massive efficiency who basically ran the school—and into Mr. Wagner's office.

The principal genuinely believed that his job was simply getting out of the way to allow teachers to teach. He mostly dealt with problems in the cafeteria—like why ten percent of the milk was always one day past its expiration date, and why did so many children have so much trouble unwrapping the butter pats so that little bits of tinfoil stuck to the floor and had to be picked up piece by small, sticky, grubby, slippery, tiny little piece, and why, oh *why* did the cook insist on creating new recipes consisting of terrifying combinations (wasabi tuna noodle casserole spring rolls and chocolate potato pie, for example) that inevitably resulted in numerous parents griping to Mr. Wagner about their children's nausea?

And now, of course, erasers.

"Come in, Lyle, it's good to see you." Mr. Wagner motioned to a chair opposite his desk. "How are things going?"

"Fine." Mudshark waited.

"For some time now, I've heard that you are good at finding things."

Mudshark nodded.

"I'm having trouble with something." Mr. Wagner looked uncomfortable. Mudshark nodded encouragingly.

Mr. Wagner hesitated, took a deep breath and then blurted:

"Alltheerasersinschoolseemtohavebeenstolen."

"I've noticed."

"It's hard not to. Half the teachers have taken to using their shirttails to wipe off the board, which makes for some uncomfortable half-clothed moments in the classroom. Another half are swiping gym towels from the locker rooms, so now we've got showers full of wet kids but no towels. Then the other half of the faculty are asking for easels and enormous pads of paper to write on, which simply isn't in my budget. Then there's the half that just keeps writing *over* everything and have you *seen* that undecipherable layer of gobbledygook on the boards in the science wing?"

"That's four halves, sir."

"It is?"

"Yes, but I see your point."

"It seems a silly concern, I know, especially given the disastrous end to the recent Death Ball tournament and the still-lost gerbil and that weird parrot in the library and don't even get me started about the faculty washroom crisis, but I wonder if you could help me find the erasers."

Mudshark smiled.

"Of course."

Mudshark went home after school, thinking about the principal's request. As soon as he entered the house, his mother whizzed past him, thrusting a sticky Sara into his arms.

"Look, lovey, would you be a dear and watch the girls for me? I have to give a presentation at the library and your father is running late at the office. The girls are doing an art project so they shouldn't be any trouble for you while you wait for Dad to get home."

Mudshark held Sara at arm's length and inventoried the damage: a piece of dog kibble was stuck in her hair, she had colored her entire right hand with purple marker and her shoes were not only mismatched but also on the wrong feet.

He looked out at the driveway and saw his mother hurrying toward the car, three tiny but perfect purple handprints on the seat of her crisp white suit skirt.

"Kara. Tara," he bellowed. "Park. Now. Move."

He set Sara down and held her purple hand as they waited for the other girls to come tearing down the hall from the playroom. He noted that Kara had the shoes that matched Sara's, Tara's dress was on backward and inside out and both of them had also colored their right hands purple. They walked out to the garage and he loaded them in the red wagon for the five-block trip to the park behind his school.

Once set free on the playground, the girls scattered, one to the sandbox, another to the gray plastic hippopotamus on its enormous spring and a third to the merry-go-round.

Mudshark sat on a bench facing the school building and eyeballed the girls as he let his mind drift, idly noticing a van pulling up to the back of the school. He came to attention when he saw a tall man carrying large, flat packages from the side door of the van to the basement door of the school. The man handled the packages carefully, one at a time, and lined them up near the door. After he'd unloaded six or seven packages, he started taking them down to the basement. The basement . . . the custodian . . .

"Don't!"

Mudshark looked over at his sisters, who were now all in the sandbox. They were each drawing with a stick, smoothing the sand down and patting the space in front of them flat before dragging the stick like a paintbrush through the sand to make lines. Tara was on her feet, waving her hands and shrieking at Kara and Sara.

"Don't wreck it! Don't wipe away my picture and draw over it!" She stomped on their pictures, and they all started crying.

Mudshark got up to deal with the girls. He looked toward the school, tipped his head and narrowed his eyes, thinking. Then he nodded and smiled. "Gotcha. I know what's been going on now."

Just then the girls tackled him, sat on him and sprinkled him with sand.

This is the principal. *Would the custodian please report to the faculty restroom with a Geiger counter, lead-lined gloves and smoked-lens goggles? Would whoever took all the erasers from all the rooms in the entire building please return them? Will the gerbil, if he's listening, please refrain from terrorizing Mr. Patterson? And Mr. Patterson, will you please stop carrying the tennis racket up and down the halls and dropping a backhand on anything that moves? Three parents have called complaining of waffle marks on their children's faces. Thank you.*

Mudshark hesitated.

It was the next morning. Mudshark stood in front of a door in the basement of the school that he had never seen opened before. A door no student had ever passed through. He raised his hand and turned the knob.

Slowly, the door opened.

He peered inside.

"It's like a museum!"

This was the custodian's room, a small work space under the stairs. The walls were covered with posters of art and with actual paintings. Small sculptures stood on tables in the corners. The room glowed with light and color. As Mudshark leaned in, he heard classical music and recognized it from music-appreciation class: Pachelbel's Canon in D Major.

The custodian turned around, startled.

"Hey!" He smiled. "People don't usually come in here."

"It's beautiful."

"That's the idea. My name's Bill. Bill Wilson. And you're . . . ?"

"Mudshark."

"Ah! The Mudshark Detective Agency. I saw the sign. Glad you like it here. I have lots of paintings and posters at home, so I take some home, bring new ones in, keep things fresh. You can't have too much beauty . . ." He trailed off, serious for a moment, then smiled. "Ever."

"Why don't you hang these in the hall, where everyone can see?"

"I think that how someone looks at art is mostly private. I don't feel it's fair to force other people to see things the way I see them. It's never right to force people . . ." Again, the serious look, then another smile. ". . . to do anything. Ever. Besides, it's safe here. The beauty."

"Safe . . . ," Mudshark said.

Bill looked at him. "Safe is a very big deal to me." He saw Mudshark's confusion. "You see . . . when I was eighteen, a college freshman, a war began and I felt I should help my country, so I joined the military and I was sent to fight. For two years, three months, twenty-one days and nine

50

hours. I saw . . . terrible things. I did some of them myself." He looked down at the floor, lost in his thoughts.

Mudshark gently cleared his throat to get Bill's attention. "Go on."

"Anyway," Bill went on, "when I got out of the service and came home, I wasn't the same. War changed me. I didn't want what I'd wanted before, college and a normal career and all that. I wanted something else."

"Peace," Mudshark guessed, and Bill nodded. "That makes sense."

"The one thing I knew was that I wanted to live in a way that could never possibly hurt another person or creature. Where I could spend the rest of my life seeking beauty. And joy.

"I didn't want to go to college, but I still wanted an education. So I read like crazy—Plato and Aristotle and Shakespeare and Sir Arthur Conan Doyle and Jane Austen and John Cheever and Dylan Thomas and Mark Twain and Hemingway—all kinds of poems and novels and plays. I traveled all over to go to museums and galleries so that I could look at paintings and sculpture—Rembrandt, Degas, Michelangelo, Jackson Pollock, Andy Warhol, Christo . . . I went to the ballet to see the choreography of Agnes de Mille and Balanchine; modern dance, too, Twyla Tharp and Merce Cunningham, and wacky new things at student festivals. I went to concerts—Mozart, Beethoven, Strauss, Vivaldi and Bach. New music, too, by young composers who were just starting out. I couldn't even list all that I studied. It was wonderful."

"A great life," Mudshark agreed.

"But still"—Bill frowned—"a person has to eat. And pay the electricity bill. And buy pants. I needed a job. But one where I could work in peace and still have time to keep up my studies. I tried jobs in hospitals, driving a bus, mowing lawns, painting houses, smoothing concrete . . . nothing really fit. Until one day I drove past the middle school. And I thought, hey! A custodian. Even the name made sense. I could be the custodian not just of the building but of the joyful things I'd found, too. It was perfect. Until . . ."

"The erasers." Mudshark took a chance and jumped into the silence. "You took them. But how do they fit into all this?"

Bill sighed. "How'd you know it was me?"

"Logic," Mudshark said. "You were the only person with access to all the rooms. But how come you did it?"

"It's kind of complicated."

Silence, except for the sound of people walking by outside.

Bill hesitated. "I hate . . . no, that's too strong a word. Let's see . . . When beauty ends, it's just so sad and meaningless."

Mudshark nodded.

"One day, a girl wrote something amazing on a blackboard when I was in the room setting up a new crayfish tank. I stopped and looked at the board. It was as vivid and . . . meaningful in its own way as any painting I'd ever seen in any museum. And then the teacher erased it."

Bill took a deep breath. "It was . . . painful. To see it vanish. And I suppose it was wrong, but I thought, you know, if that eraser wasn't there, it wouldn't be so easy to wipe away."

"What was erased?"

"She wrote, 'I can hear the color green and taste the color blue.' "

"That was it?"

"It doesn't sound like much. But think of it! She can hear and taste colors—how incredible! And then the idea was gone, lost, and no one else can ever see it and wonder like I did. Another time, I watched some kids at the blackboard doing math together. They were so excited that they'd solved the problem—I hated to see that wiped away. So I took those erasers. And then I couldn't stop."

"I see what you mean," Mudshark said. He thought. "But . . . that's funny, though, 'cause I like looking at a clean blackboard. It's ready for anyone to draw or write anything. Like it's . . . waiting for a new idea and everything is possible."

Bill nodded slowly. "Maybe you're right about that."

Mudshark thought again. "And then," he said, "people *expect* a blackboard to be erased. They don't mind. And erasing mistakes is good, because you can keep going, trying to find the solution. And, you know, solving things, that's kind of beautiful. Well, I think so anyway. I like figuring things out."

Bill turned to put in a new CD and Mudshark noticed a small box on top of the speaker with a hole cut out like a little cave. A set of tiny whiskers poked out and he heard a soft scratching sound from within. Bill glanced at him.

Mudshark grinned. "I won't say anything to Mr. Patterson if you won't."

"He likes the music," Bill said. "I think it's soothing after his . . . misadventures on the run. I kept him here to fatten him up. He was half starved after being lost for so long. Sometimes he goes off exploring." He chuckled. "Poor Mr. Patterson."

"Oh, I don't know. I bet he kind of likes the excitement. Everybody noticed that Mr. Patterson was pretty bored with school after he came back from that wilderness camp last summer. Now he's all charged up."

"He sure is. I had to rescue him from a vent this morning—his leg was stuck. This job is more interesting every day."

"That's one way to look at this school."

"So about the erasers," Bill continued. "You make a good point. I never thought about it that way before. But I suppose you'll have to tell Mr. Wagner that I took them. I like my job and I'd hate to lose it because I stole some erasers. They have a zero-tolerance policy on theft in this school district."

Mudshark thought. "He only asked me to *find* them. He never said he wanted to know who had taken them or why. If I put them back, I bet he won't care about who did it. He's got bigger stuff to deal with."

"Yeah, the faculty restroom and that weird parrot in the library." Bill laughed but then looked at Mudshark, who was scowling. "What's the matter?"

"The bird's got a really big mouth," Mudshark said. "And he's not afraid to use it. You taking the erasers is just the kind of thing he would notice. I've got to stop him from figuring it out and telling the whole school! Fast."

9

This is the principal. *The area within fifteen feet of the door of the faculty restroom, defined by yellow warning tape, has been declared a hazardous material area. Do not enter this taped area, and when passing please refrain from looking directly at the bright light coming from beneath the door. Thank you. Oh, yes, and the gerbil has allegedly been cornered in the science lab room. Mr. Patterson will report specifics later. Thank you.*

While Mudshark was wondering how he could return all the erasers without getting Bill in trouble or arousing any further suspicion, Helen Cartwright came to ask him to find her missing cat, Toby.

In Mudshark's opinion, Toby was more than a little mean. Mudshark had seen the scratches on Helen's arms. Toby was an ankle nipper, too. Mudshark couldn't help noticing that Toby's mood had become worse after Helen had turned twelve. He was no longer the apple of Helen's eye.

Helen, Mudshark knew from sitting near her in the cafeteria at lunch, liked to talk about boys and more boys and still more boys and who was a geek and who was not a geek and which lip gloss looked best when talking to boys.

Mudshark guessed that, in addition to being cranky, Toby was also bored out of his mind living with Helen. Mudshark was certainly bored out of his mind just sitting near her during lunch.

A bored cat, Mudshark knew, is a leaving cat.

Later that day, he was in the grocery store and saw Helen's neighbor Mrs. Downside. She was giving very specific instructions to the butcher about trimming the fat from a piece of sirloin. But Mudshark knew that Mrs. Downside was a vegan, because when she'd broken her hip the winter before, Mudshark's mother had volunteered him to do her grocery shopping. He looked in Mrs. Downside's cart. Aha! Cat treats. From the looks of her new grocery shopping habits, Toby had found himself a new home. Mrs. Downside hadn't had any pets last winter.

Mudshark volunteered to help Mrs. Downside home with her groceries. When they got to her house, Mudshark sat on the front porch with her, drinking lemonade. He watched Toby eat sirloin that she hand-fed to him while he reclined on a purple satin cushion that had his new name, Mr. Cuddles, embroidered on it in gold letters. Then Mrs. Downside brushed Toby's coat with a soft-bristled brush.

"I special-ordered this from the Precious and Pampered Pet Web site for Mr. Cuddles. He enjoys a good brushing. Poor thing; he obviously never had a loving home before."

"He's a really nice cat, Mrs. Downside." Mudshark got up. "Thanks for the lemonade."

"Thank you, Lyle, for helping me with my

groceries," she said, brushing the surprisingly docile Mr. Cuddles.

Mudshark trotted down the street to Helen's house to report his findings.

"You might get him back," Mudshark told Helen, "but it would be an uphill fight to keep him. Mrs. Downside has time to sit with him, but you have school. You could bring him home by force, but the first time he got out . . . They seem like they belong together, actually; they were both bor—I mean, lonely."

Helen nodded. "You know, Mudshark," she said, "actually, I'm just as glad that he's found another home. I mean, I love him and all, but, well, have you noticed that he's kind of mean?" She absent-mindedly patted the scratches on her arms. "But I need him for a science project that Betty Crimper and I are doing in lab tomorrow. She was working on building a better mousetrap. Or, wait, no, was it creating a new kind of catnip? I'm not very good at science and so I haven't really paid attention. Bringing Toby as a visual aid for our oral presentation was my only responsibility for the project we're doing tomorrow. Can you believe I had to get special permission from the principal to bring an animal onto school property? I mean, we had crayfish in every classroom and now a gerbil on the loose and that weird parrot in the library and . . . what is it?"

Mudshark had leapt to his feet. "That's it!" He beamed at Helen. "Don't worry about bringing the cat to school for your science project; I'll speak to Mrs. Downside about borrowing him. Kyle and I need to use Toby for a little while after school, too. And then—could you and Betty help me out? I'm working on an experiment of my own."

10

This is the principal. *Please refrain from distracting the hazmat crew the government has sent in. They are working to contain the dangerous material in the faculty restroom, sealing it in lead-lined containers before sending it to appropriate government agencies for classification and neutralizing. Oh, and Mr. Patterson was last seen heading up into the overhead heating and air-conditioning ducts in pursuit of the gerbil, so refrain from becoming distracted by the thumping and banging overhead. Thank you.*

Mudshark sat at the library table the next day, looking at the parrot and listening to the low buzz around him; everyone was talking about the missing erasers, the art posters that had suddenly started to appear all over the school and the classical music wafting out of the custodian's room.

Mudshark noticed that the parrot, like him, seemed to listen to *everything*, cocking his head and closing his eyes, almost as if he were filing the words away. Like some sort of feather-covered computer.

"Hmmm . . . ," Mudshark said aloud, "feathers." He closed his own eyes, remembering. A few tiny green feathers in the boys' room, a stray feather fluttering down the hallway . . . He opened his eyes, homing in on the open transom above the library door. He reached out and jiggled the door of the birdcage. It popped open.

Aha! So that was how the parrot collected information.

Mudshark looked over at Ms. Underdorf, who had her back to the room, her nose in a book. He stole a peek around the room, where everyone was deep into either whispered gossip or homework.

Although improbable, it *was* likely that no one noticed the bird getting out of his cage and out of the library to stealthily patrol the halls of the school from time to time. Especially if it happened when the school was empty.

Like Mudshark, the bird paid attention to details and gathered information in a way that no one, not even Mudshark himself, had noticed.

"Well done, my good bird, well done," Mudshark whispered approvingly. "But I'm the big fish around here, and more important, I can't let you see everything; that's no good."

The parrot belched, ruffled his feathers and, with his beak, picked at the loose door of his cage. "Going. Walk. Shhhh."

Mudshark quickly tied the cage shut with a piece of string he pulled out of his backpack. He knew that it was just a matter of time before the parrot noticed that the custodian was the person putting up the art posters and was responsible for piping classical music into the library, and then heard the talk about the erasers. Sooner or later the parrot might blurt out everything he knew about the custodian. And Mudshark didn't want a person who believed in beauty and peace in a zero-tolerance world to get in any trouble because of some bird. The delicate balance of his school must be kept.

But short of physical intervention—say, letting a Tasmanian devil into the library one night—how to shut the parrot up?

Mudshark listened to music drifting up the stairs from the basement and stared at the parrot and considered his options, and the field of possible partners and how he might most effectively utilize their particular gifts and strengths.

He let the energy in his mind jump around: the parrot . . . Kyle's magic . . . Bill's beautiful workroom and Ms. Underdorf's library . . . Betty Crimper's science projects . . . Helen and Toby/Mr. Cuddles . . . the cook's scary and disgusting recipes . . . the faculty restroom. Stop! Even Mudshark shied away from the thought of the faculty restroom.

He knew that the practice of free thinking, allowing random thoughts to drift through his mind undirected, would eventually lead him to the solution.

Operation Eraser Return.

He opened his eyes and said quietly, so that only the parrot could hear, "You, my fine feathered friend, are a problem about to be solved."

This is the principal. *I cannot stress strongly enough that, for your own safety and per the restrictions of Homeland Security, to whom, by the way, we'd like to offer a warm welcome, please refrain from going anywhere near the faculty restroom. Oh, and great news about Mr. Patterson. While he still hasn't caught the gerbil, his application for another summer of teaching wilderness camp has just been approved. Way to go, Mr. Patterson! Thank you.*

Kyle Robertson was outside the library door, hopping from one foot to the other. "So, Mudshark, what's the plan? Operation Eraser Return: that sounds like a good new trick!"

Betty Crimper stood next to Bill the custodian. Helen Cartwright held Toby/Mr. Cuddles's cat carrier. Ms. Underdorf was on the other side of Mudshark, eyeing the large cardboard box next to Bill.

The school day was over and all the teachers were in a meeting with the school board. The entire building was quiet and, except for the faculty in the cafeteria and Mudshark's team outside the library, deserted.

"Bill here," Mudshark said, "for reasons of his own, is responsible for the temporary removal of all the classroom erasers. We need to return them this afternoon. Fast. And we need to make sure the parrot doesn't find out anything about this because he'll tell and then Bill will get in trouble."

Helen, Kyle and Betty nodded and Ms. Underdorf looked at Bill sympathetically.

"Let's work together to make the parrot dislike answering questions about *custodian* or *eraser*, so that, if anybody ever does ask him about those two things, he won't know the answer."

"Isn't he psychic, though?" Helen asked.

"No. He's just . . . observant. I want to make sure he doesn't observe the wrong things. Oh, and we also need to curb his wandering ways at the same time. So can you help me?"

"Where do we start?" Kyle said.

"With the cat."

"You don't want Toby to, you know, like . . . hurt . . . the parrot or anything, do you?" Helen looked a little sick.

"No, of course not, we just distract the parrot with Toby. I'm sure the parrot hasn't seen too many cats before and he'll be curious and want to investigate. We go in the library, show the parrot the cat and then get the bird to follow Toby to the lab, where Betty can release some of her Odors to Repel at the same time that everyone says *custodian* and *erasers* over and over. That will plant a negative association in the parrot's head. With leaving his cage, too."

"And cats," Kyle said.

"Can parrots smell? I feel like I should know

70

that," Ms. Underdorf said. Mudshark noticed Bill patting her shoulder kindly.

Mudshark went on, "I read that the apparatus for detecting odors is present in the nasal passages of all birds."

"But we're not *hurting* him, right?" Helen peered doubtfully at Toby/Mr. Cuddles.

"No! Think of it as aversion therapy. One whiff of Betty's formula should cure the bird of any interest in erasers and of his wandering tendencies. Maybe for life. Meanwhile, what he doesn't see, he can't tell."

They all nodded.

"All right, then," Betty said, "I'll go get set up. My science is stronger than something covered with feathers and a brain the size of a peanut." Betty squared her shoulders and trotted off to the lab.

Helen, carrying Toby/Mr. Cuddles, followed Mudshark into the library. Mudshark removed the night cover from the parrot's cage, untied the string he'd left there before and set the door slightly ajar. When he saw the parrot fix his gaze on the cat, he nodded to Helen, who began walking slowly toward the door, looking back to make sure she had the bird's attention. The parrot squawked and said, "Hey, babe, wait up," before nudging his door open and hopping out of the cage, onto the table and then down to the floor. Mudshark watched the bird jump and flap after Helen and Toby/Mr. Cuddles before he turned back to Kyle, Ms. Underdorf and Bill.

Ms. Underdorf was showing Bill the sketches for the new library, scheduled to be completed in five years. ". . . After, of course the athletic center is updated three more times and the soccer field has been AstroTurfed."

Bill looked at the sketches and listened to her gush about the new automated book-handling system and the electronic blackboards—

"Wait!" Mudshark and Bill said at the same time. "Electronic blackboards?"

"Yes!" Ms. Underdorf said. "The library will be equipped with electronic blackboards instead of the regular old-fashioned chalkboards. There are styluses that can draw or write in different colors, and everything, every last mark, can all be saved on a computer."

"It doesn't have to be erased?" Bill looked awestruck and Mudshark thoughtful.

"It *can* be erased, but whatever was there can be saved just like it was written on a computer, and brought back anytime you like. And if it works in the library they're going to incorporate it throughout the whole school system—that's the last item on to-day's board meeting with the faculty. It makes me crazy, but the library somehow always comes in last. I mean, really, is it *necessary* to have an Olympic-size curling rink before the library gets anything? Does the library have to fight for every penny?"

"I hear you," Bill said.

"That"—Mudshark grabbed Kyle's arm—"might be changing. As soon as I can get Kyle to practice his misdirection on a couple of school board members . . . In the meantime, though, Bill, you and Ms. Underdorf take the box of erasers and head off to the west wing. Betty and Helen and Toby will need about half an hour with the parrot in the science lab on the east side. Meanwhile, Kyle and I head to the board meeting in the cafeteria.

"After tonight," Mudshark added, "This school will never be the same!"

"Neither will the parrot," Kyle said, "especially after he gets a whiff of Betty's invention."

12

The yellow tape around the faculty bathroom was dragging on the floor and a clanging sound came from inside as Mudshark and Kyle headed to the cafeteria. Mudshark, after giving him last-minute in-structions, sent Kyle along to the cafeteria without him. "I'll meet up with you!"

Mudshark gingerly poked his head in at the bathroom door and looked around. Mr. Thomas, the science teacher, stood in front of a row of sinks, a clothespin on his nose and a surgical mask across the lower part of his face, dumping a bucket into one of the sinks. A hissing cloud rose and sur-rounded him.

Mudshark coughed from the stench and Mr. Thomas turned toward the sound. "Oh, Mudshark"—his voice was muffled by the mask—"uh, hm, well . . . It's that Betty Crimper! I don't even know what she does in my lab but that young woman comes up with the most perplexing, noxious concoctions. I know, based on the raw materials she has to work with, that it can't be truly hazardous, but she does stink up my lab." He looked around nervously. "You won't tell anyone, will you? I don't mean to discourage Betty's powerful scientific curiosity, and she's getting ready for a big competition this weekend, and I'd hate to put her off her research when we're so close to the end of her . . . um, experiments."

"I won't say a word, Mr. Thomas. Are your eyebrows going to grow back, though?"

"Oh, it's temporary. I've lost and regrown them a few times. Hazard of the profession."

Mudshark waved goodbye to Mr. Thomas and headed off to the cafeteria. He stopped at a corner. Peering in one direction along the hallway, he saw

Helen and Betty returning to the library. Betty carried the parrot. She and Helen still wore their protective goggles and face masks. Mudshark could hear a faint gagging sound coming from the cat carrier that Helen held, and the parrot, he noticed, had tucked his head under one of his wings. Mudshark glanced the other way and saw Bill and Ms. Underdorf scurrying in and out of classrooms, tossing erasers down the hall to each other as their box of stolen goods got lighter and lighter and the classrooms were once again fully stocked.

Mudshark smiled, nodded and ran to the cafeteria.

He arrived in the middle of Kyle's impromptu magic show for the school board members. Kyle was zipping several tricks past them—quarters, pulled from behind ears, winking in the light, silk scarves slipped from board members' sleeves, bunches of flowers emerging from one woman's purse—and once they were in what he'd called "observational confusion," he threw in a side-focus, the magician's form of hypnosis, he explained, speaking fast and moving his hands quickly, so that whenever they heard the word *athletic department* they would think *new library* and *electronic blackboards*.

Mudshark grinned and flashed a thumbs-up to Kyle.

13

A sign on the library door read: ELECTRONIC BLACK-
BOARDS ARRIVING ANY DAY NOW!

Meanwhile Kyle's magic show had also affected
the cook, who had been making crazy recipes that
left everyone gagging and dizzy. She was inadver-
tently misdirected so severely that she began to try
regular menu plans, much to the relief of the entire
student body. And the school nurse.

Ms. Underdorf and Bill were seen leaving the
school grounds together each day after classes, talking about books and art, hurrying to get a bite to eat
before heading to a play or concert.

Mr. Wagner was very grateful for the returned

erasers. When he thanked Mudshark, he said, "Who took them, where you found them and how they were returned can be your little secret—no more questions. I'm just so happy that the erasers are back and the faculty washroom is less toxic and the cook is creating food that doesn't make people see colors anymore. Look—her first new menu!" He held it out and Mudshark read:

~~Prune Liver Surprise~~ Cottage Cheese
~~Franks n' Brussels Sprouts~~ Grilled Cheese
~~Salami Mint Whip~~ Yogurt

"It's a tad . . . milky," Mr. Wagner said. "But it's a start. She's returning to her roots—she grew up on a dairy farm."

Yes, things were getting back to normal. Even the triplets had learned to dress themselves and sit quietly for upwards of thirty seconds at a time.

In truth, though, after the excitement of the erasers and the parrot, Mudshark was getting a little bored.

Until.

AFTERWORD

This is the principal. *I am pleased to report that each and every classroom is fully stocked with erasers. The faculty restroom is safe for human use. That being said, would the custodian please report to the faculty restroom with a plunger and a mop? Today's hot lunch offering is cheese pizza, applesauce, green beans, chocolate pudding and two-percent milk. Our own Betty Crimper has taken first place in the Interscholastic Science Fair that was held this past weekend—way to go, Betty! Please direct your attention to the new electronic blackboards in the library; we will shortly be replacing* *the crayfish tanks in each classroom with these boards. I know that we are all sorry to hear that due to the custodian's allergy attacks, our library mascot, that weird . . . the parrot, has had to find another home. We are pleased, though, that Mrs. Downside has taken him in. Last of all, would Lyle Williams report immediately to the principal's office?*

Mr. Wagner closed his door and looked at Mudshark with desperation and said, "You did so well on the eraser business . . ."

Mudshark waited.

"I wonder if you could help me with another problem."

Mudshark nodded.

"We can't seem to locate Mr. Patterson. As near as we can figure, he's lost somewhere in the west wing, where he was last heard rumbling around up in the ductwork, hunting for the gerbil. He must be coming out, because somebody has been eating the sandwiches we put out each night, but we can't pin him down long enough to get him to emerge and start teaching again. I don't suppose you would mind looking into it, would you? Please? We must get our eighth-grade English teacher back in the classroom and out of the ductwork."

Well, Mudshark thought as he headed for the west wing, this should be interesting. . . .

ABOUT THE AUTHOR

Gary Paulsen is the distinguished author of many critically acclaimed books for young people, including three Newbery Honor books: *The Winter Room*, *Hatchet*, and *Dogsong*. His novel *The Haymeadow* received the Western Writers of America Golden Spur Award. Among his Random House books are *Lawn Boy*; *The Legend of Bass Reeves*; *The Amazing Life of Birds*; *The Time Hackers*; *Molly McGinty Has a Really Good Day*; *The Quilt* (a companion to *Alida's Song* and *The Cookcamp*); *The Glass Café*; *How Angel Peterson Got His Name*; *Guts: The True Stories Behind* Hatchet *and the Brian Books*; *The Beet Fields*; *Soldier's Heart*; *Brian's Return*, *Brian's Winter*, and *Brian's Hunt* (companions to *Hatchet*); *Father Water, Mother Woods*; and five books about Francis Tucket's adventures in the Old West. Gary Paulsen has also published fiction and nonfiction for adults, as well as picture books illustrated by his wife, the painter Ruth Wright Paulsen. Their most recent book is *Canoe Days*. The Paulsens live in Alaska and New Mexico.

You can visit Gary Paulsen on the Web at www.garypaulsen.com.